For Laura. Why? It just is - L.C.
For Abigail and Penguin - T.R.

written by Lindsay Camp
illustrated by Tony Ross

G. P. Putnam's Sons
New York

There was one thing Lily did that drove her dad mad.

Actually, it wasn't a thing she *did*.

It was a thing she said.

She said it all the time.

She said it first thing in the morning.

It's time you were dressed.

Why?

She said it at breakfast time.

She said it when they went shopping.

Let's not forget to buy garbage bags.

Why?

She said it when her dad read her a story.

And, of course, she said it at bedtime.

Usually, Lily's dad did his best to explain.

Because it rained all last night.

Why?

Because there were lots of big black clouds full of tiny drops of water.

Why?

Because . . . well, there just were, Lily.

There just were!

But sometimes, when he was a bit tired, he'd just get cranky.

Then, one Friday, something rather unusual happened.

Lily was playing in the sandbox in the park.

Suddenly, Lily's dad stopped and looked upwards. So did Lily.
And so did everybody else in the park.

Lily was too astonished to say anything. After all, she'd never seen a gigantic Thargon spaceship before.

The Thargon spaceship came lower, and then it landed in the park, right next to the sandbox.

Everybody stood and stared. The doors of the spaceship slid open

and out squelched several Thargons.

They didn't look very friendly.

The most important Thargon oozed forward.

Everyone started to tremble. Everyone except Lily, that is.

Why?

WHY?
Because that is our
mission, of course.

Because destroying
puny planets brings
glory to the mighty
Thargon Empire.

Because . . . well,
because our Great Leader,
the Imperial Tharg, says so.

Because . . . he just does,
Small Female Earthling,
he just does. Hmmm . . .

The chief Thargon turned to his friends. He looked thoughtful.

Lily and her dad and all the other people watched as they talked together in Thargish for quite a long time.

Then the chief Thargon slithered forward again, and spoke to Lily.

Lily was just about to say something

but her dad put his hand over her mouth, just in time.

BYE!
Have a nice day. Sorry
to have troubled you.

That night at bedtime, when he'd finished reading her a story,

Lily's dad gave her an extra big hug.

And then he promised he'd never get cranky with her again,
no matter how often she asked him why.

I was very proud
of you in the park
today.

Why?

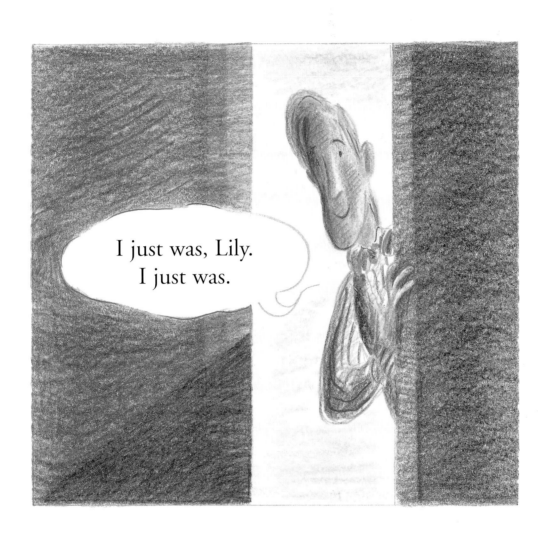

Porque Warum why Per
nach Pourquoi why?
Waarum hvorfor warum nach
Proč Perché why?
hvorfor Pourquoi nach Proč Perché why?
Proč nach Porque Perché why?
Pourquoi nach Proč why? why?
Waarum Proč why dlaczego hvorfor niçin Pourquoi
Proč niçin warum why Proč
why niçin yiari hvorfor perqué
Proč pourquoi nach? cur why
niçin Proč Pourquoi Pourquoi niçin
Pourquoi hvorfor nach niçin why
Pam nach Perqué cur why
dlaczego pourquoi why pourquoi why
nach hvorfor
why Pourquoi Proč Pam why yiari Perqué
warum why Waarum Pam
niçin nach yiari why
perqué why Почему Perqué why
why dlaczego Pourquoi niçin niçin
why Pam Pourquoi dlaczego cur